Dora and the Unicorn King

Adapted by Molly Reisner
Based on the teleplay "King Unicornio" by Rosemary Contreras
Illustrated by David Aikins

🦖 A GOLDEN BOOK • NEW YORK

© 2011 Viacom International Inc. All rights reserved. Published in the United States by Golden Books, an imprint of Random House Children's Books, a division of Random House, Inc., 1745 Broadway, New York, NY 10019, and in Canada by Random House of Canada Limited, Toronto. Golden Books, A Golden Book, A Little Golden Book, the G colophon, and the distinctive gold spine are registered trademarks of Random House, Inc. Nickelodeon, Nick Jr., Dora the Explorer, and all related titles, logos, and characters are trademarks of Viacom International Inc.
www.randomhouse.com/kids
ISBN: 978-0-375-87226-6
Printed in the United States of America
20 19 18 17 16 15 14 13 12

While walking through the forest one day, Dora and Boots saw a big, beautiful rainbow in the sky. Suddenly, their friend Unicornio came racing down the side! He was giving his friends a ride.

A rabbit holding a scroll hopped up to Unicornio.

"'Because you are kind, strong, smart, and brave, the citizens of the forest have picked you to be king,'" the rabbit read. "'You must get to the Castle in the Enchanted Forest so you can be crowned!'"

Unicornio was worried. He didn't think he was kind, strong, smart, or brave.

Dora hugged Unicornio. "Boots and I will show you that you are all those things!"

The three friends journeyed to the beautiful Enchanted Forest.

"How will we find the Castle?" Boots asked.
"Let's ask Map!" said Dora.
Map said that they had to go through the Riddle Tree, then past the Volcano. Then they would see the Castle.

On the way to the Riddle Tree, the friends
met five elves picking peaches. All the elves
had peaches in their baskets . . . except Littlest
Elf. He stretched and jumped, but he couldn't
reach a peach!

"Want a boost?" Unicornio asked.

The little elf climbed up Unicornio's neck. Now he could reach lots of peaches!

"Thank you," said Littlest Elf. "You're very kind."

The other elves agreed. Unicornio was happy to discover that he WAS kind!

Dora, Boots, and Unicornio traveled on. They finally found the Riddle Tree. An owl sat on one of its branches.

"No one is as smart as I!" bragged Owl. He challenged Unicornio to a riddle contest.

The Riddle Tree asked, "Who lives in a castle
and rules over all that can be seen—"
"A king!" interrupted Owl. But he was wrong.
"A ruler is not always a king," the Riddle
Tree said. "Sometimes she's a . . ."
Unicornio took a moment to think.

"A queen!" Unicornio answered. He was right!
"You're really smart," said Owl.

Just then, a golden tunnel opened up in the Riddle Tree's trunk! Unicornio, Dora, and Boots waved goodbye and entered the tunnel.

At the end of the tunnel, the friends found the Volcano. The Volcano rumbled. Puffs of smoke rose from the top . . . and a dragon flew out!

    As Boots was running away from the
dragon, he tripped on a rock!
    "Uh-oh, the dragon is going to get Boots!"
cried Dora. Unicornio remembered that he had
a special way to protect his friends.

Unicornio stood in front of Dora and Boots.
"My magic horn will keep the dragon back!"
he said. He stomped his hooves, and magic
sparkles came out of his horn!

Dora and Boots helped by stomping, too.
The sparkles made a powerful shield.

The dragon bounced off the shield and flew away!

"Unicornio, thanks for protecting me," said Boots. "You're so brave!"

Unicornio was very proud that he had helped his friends.

Dora could see the Castle in the distance.
She and Boots climbed onto Unicornio's back.
He galloped as fast as he could.

Unicornio had already proved to himself that he was kind, smart, and brave. But he still had to prove that he was strong. Only then would Unicornio feel ready to be crowned king!

On the way to the Castle, Rabbit stopped Unicornio. "I need your help! Squirrel fell into the water!" he cried.

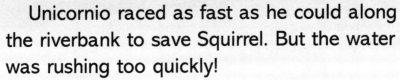

Unicornio raced as fast as he could along the riverbank to save Squirrel. But the water was rushing too quickly!

"We need something to help pull Squirrel out of the water," said Boots.

Dora checked Backpack and found the perfect thing—a life preserver! She threw the ring around Squirrel.

"We're going to have to be super strong!" yelled Dora.

"I'm strong!" Unicornio said, and he tied the rope around his body.

Unicornio pulled and pulled . . . and finally pulled Squirrel out of the water to safety!

The forest creatures cheered.
"You're really strong! Thanks for helping me!" said Squirrel.

All the fairies, elves, and animals of the Enchanted Forest arrived at the Castle wearing their finest clothes. They thanked Unicornio for being kind, smart, brave, and strong.

Dora was very proud of Unicornio.

"Now do you see that you are ready to be king?" she asked.

"Yes," Unicornio said. "I AM ready!"

"I now declare you king!" announced Rabbit, putting a crown on Unicornio's head. Trumpets tooted and everyone celebrated.

Dora and Boots cheered, "Hip, hip, hooray for King Unicornio!"